Cambria

In memory of my mother,
who would have been so proud.

For Booth.

Special thanks to Victoria Rock, Kendra Marcus,
and to Beth for being on a ferry on Lake Como.

ISBN 0-590-42594-3

Copyright © 1994 by Nina Laden.
All rights reserved. Published by Scholastic Inc., 555 Broadway, New York, NY 10012, by
arrangement with Chronicle Books.

12 11 10 9 8 7 6 5 4 3 2   6 7 8 9/9 0 1/0

Printed in the U.S.A.   08

First Scholastic printing, January 1996

THE NIGHT I FOLLOWED THE DOG

WORDS AND PICTURES BY NINA LADEN

SCHOLASTIC INC.
NEW YORK TORONTO LONDON AUCKLAND SYDNEY

I have a dog. Nothing exotic or special, just an ordinary dog. In fact, I always thought he was a boring dog. What I mean is, he can Fetch, ROLL OVER, and shake hands, but mostly he sleeps and EATS.

I used to think that our next-door neighbors had the best dog in the w🌍rld. Their dog can 𝓢ing and change the channels on the 📺. Their dog always wins **MEDALS** 🎖 in obedience school. But I don't think their dog is so great now — not since the night I followed **MY** dog.

Every night, I let my dog out, and he runs off into the darkness with his tail **wagging**. The next morning I let him in, and he heads straight for the food bowl. But one morning I knew something was **FUNNY** when I opened the door a little bit earlier than usual, and I saw my dog jump out of a **LIMOUSINE** . . . wearing a tuxedo.

Before I could look twice, he **DISAPPEARED** into the backyard. I opened the kitchen door and *whistled.* When he came into the house he was the same as he always is, **hungry**. I really wasn't sure that I believed what I had seen, so that night I decided to follow him.

I wore DARK CLOTHING, so I wouldn't be noticed, and I left my bicycle near the door, so I'd have it close by. When I let the dog out, I slipped out, too. I took out the garbage, so he wouldn't suspect anything. The dog went straight to his doghouse. I saw a light go on inside. **SLOWLY**, I snuck around the backyard, and peeked into the doghouse.

This was not the doghouse that I had helped build. Inside, there was a living room, a bathroom, and a **HUGE** closet full of Fancy clothes. The dog was in the bathroom. He was wearing a tuxedo and **Fumbling** with the bow tie. When he came out, he casually walked out of the doghouse, across the yard, and down the street.

I grabbed my bicycle and followed him. Two blocks later, I saw a LIMOUSINE pull over. The dog got in, and the car took off. I started pedaling **FASTER**. The car headed across town. I thought I would lose them, but luckily* they were stopped by a few red lights.

After a while, I found myself in a part of town that I had never seen before. The buildings all seemed to be empty, and it was very quiet. The limousine stopped. I hid and watched my dog get out. He DISAPPEARED into a building, and the limousine pulled away.

There was nothing on the outside of the building, just two **BRASS** fire hydrants on either side of the entrance. I opened the door. At the end of the hall there was a **NEON** sign that said "The Doghouse." I crept closer. It looked like some kind of club. I decided to get a **CLOSER** look.

The moment I opened the door two **MEAN** looking bulldogs appeared and said, "You can't come in here!" I didn't know what to say, so I said, "B-but, b-but I saw my dog ... I mean, I think my dog's in here." Just then, my dog walked over and said, "It's okay, boys, he's with me." The bulldogs said, "Sure, **Boss**. Whatever you say, **Boss**."

For a minute that seemed like forever, I waited. Then my dog said, "I knew you would find out eventually. Well, now you know. This is my place." I looked around. Finally, I asked, "What is this place?" My dog said, "This? This is a place where dogs come after a hard day. It's a place where we can **relax**. It's a place where we can talk about our problems with the MAILMAN, or with the **poodle** next door."

"See all the sofas? We can *sit* on the sofas here. We can get treats without having to ʀᴇᴛʀɪᴇᴠᴇ, ʀᴏʟʟ ᴏᴠᴇʀ, or play dead. And if we want to chew on a shoe or CHASE OUR TAIL, no one will stop us. We have no masters here, no *leashes*, and no rolled up newspapers. This? This is a place where dogs can be dogs."

We sat down. A cocker spaniel came by and asked me if I would like a bowl of water, or some BISCUITS. Little by little, dogs of all **KINDS** started coming in. Some danced, some TALKED. They all looked at me a little funny, but when they saw who I was with, they smiled, and shook my hand.

At one point, my dog waved to an afghan with a camera. She came over to our table and took a Picture of us together. Being with my dog made me feel like a movie star.

Just when I was really starting to enjoy myself, I looked at my watch. I told my dog I had to leave, or I'd get in **TROUBLE**. He nodded. I think he was about to say something, but a **Glamorous** greyhound grabbed his paw and whisked him onto the dance floor. As he was getting up, he tossed me the **PHOTO** of the two of us. Then he bowed slightly and disappeared into the **CROWD**.

It was way past my bedtime. As I pedaled home into the COOL night, I thought to myself, "Now I'm really going to be in the doghouse." But then again, that might not be so bad.

THE END